# Princess Twinkle's Magic Dress

igloobooks

Long ago, a **wicked** queen called Morlag cast an **evil** spell on a king and his daughter, Princess Twinkle. Morlag locked the king in a dungeon and made Twinkle her servant. Under Morlag's spell, the palace became a **gloomy**, miserable place.

One day, Twinkle hid and listened to the queen, as she sat on her throne.

"How **clever** of me to cast this spell and make Princess Twinkle my servant," said Morlag, **cackling** wickedly.

Twinkle **crept** out of the palace
and **ran** to the edge of the
forest to sit by the river.
"I **wish** Morlag would
disappear," she sighed.

"I have to break her spell
and make the palace a **happy** place again."

Just then, Twinkle noticed something **sparkling** in the sunlight.
Forest fairies led her to a **dazzling dress** that lay among the flowers.

"It's **beautiful,**" said Twinkle, slipping into the glittering, pink dress. She ran back to the palace to show everybody her **magical** discovery.

Twinkle went through the palace gardens, so Morlag wouldn't see her. It made Twinkle very **sad** to see how neglected the gardens were. **"Morlag's spell is getting worse,"** she said. **"I wish the gardens were beautiful again."**

Suddenly, the dress began to **glow.** Glittering light appeared and the garden began to **sparkle.** Flowers bloomed, brambles uncurled and water burst from the fountain. **"Wow! The dress makes wishes come true,"** said Twinkle, excitedly.

Twinkle wanted to show Cook her magic dress, so she **quietly** crept into the palace kitchen. Broken plates lay all around and a foul, gloopy stew **bubbled** on the table.

**"Morlag always has the finest food, but we have to eat SLOP,"** said Cook, sadly.

"I **wish** the kitchen was the happy place it used to be," said Twinkle. **Sparkles** of light drifted out of her dress. The broken plates flew back together and lots of **delicious** food appeared from out of nowhere. Everything was sparkling again. "**Thank you!**" cried Cook.

Next, Twinkle went to the ballroom. The royal musicians were playing **awful**, screeching music on their broken instruments. **"Please play like you did before!"** cried Twinkle. The musicians shook their heads. **"We can't,"** they replied, sadly. **"The queen's spell makes us play like this all day long."**

"I **wish** we had some lovely music," said Twinkle. Her dress began to glow. The instruments **gleamed** like new and the musicians played beautiful music again. The servants were so **happy.** They clapped and sang and soon forgot all about Morlag.

Morlag **marched** into the ballroom. Everybody shrank in fear.

**"What IS this?"** she hissed. **"You must only play the music that I want to hear. This is my palace and you will OBEY me!"**

There was a terrible silence and then Twinkle stepped forward. **"No, we won't!"** she said.

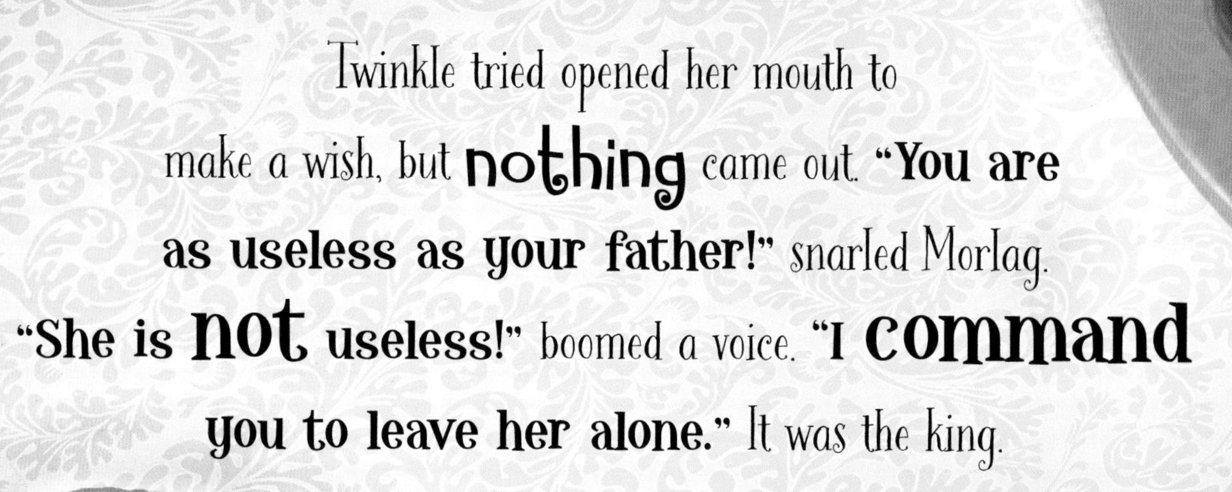

Twinkle tried opened her mouth to make a wish, but **nothing** came out. **"You are as useless as your father!"** snarled Morlag. **"She is NOT useless!"** boomed a voice. **"I command you to leave her alone."** It was the king. He had escaped from the dungeon.

**"Dad!"** cried Twinkle, running into her father's arms.

The queen was **furious** that the king had escaped.

**"This is my palace, Morlag,"** said the king.

**"Leave us alone!"**

Morlag's eyes turned a deep shade of **red.**

She **snatched** a wand from her hair and pointed it at Twinkle and the king. **"Get out of my palace, or I will turn you to stone,"** she said, with a hideous **cackle.**

Twinkle **bravely** walked up to Morlag.

**"I wish you would disappear!"** she cried.

A **spiral** of **sparkles** slowly drifted out of her dress.

"Nooooo!" cried Morlag, as the swirling spiral surrounded her.

She was pulled into the **glistening**, bright light. **Suddenly**, Twinkle's dress stopped glowing and the magical spiral faded away. Morlag had disappeared **forever.**

Finally, Morlag's wicked spell was broken. The palace was filled with **happiness** again. **"It is my command that we have the biggest celebration this palace has ever seen,"** said the king. Everyone **cheered** and danced the night away.

Twinkle had one last wish.

**"I wish we will always be happy in our palace,"** she said.

The dress no longer glowed, but Twinkle didn't mind. She knew that from now on, her wishes would **always** come true.

Everyone in the kingdom lived **happily ever after.**